To Tom
Through mist, rain, and snow
just this once
forever, and again . . .

In warm memory of my friends Marge and Linda
and my dad, whose melting snow
brought this story to life

Story copyright © 2008 by Diane Keyes. Illustrations © 2008 by Helen Stevens.
All rights reserved.
ISBN: 978-0-89272-710-0

Library of Congress Cataloging-in-Publication Data

Keyes, Diane.
 The magic of the snowpeople / by Diane Keyes ; illustrated by Helen
Stevens.
     p. cm.
 Summary: During a particularly long winter, residents of a small
northwoods community build a village of snowpeople that brings joy to
visitors from far and near, and when the sculptures begin to melt an elder
explains that their spirit will live on throughout the seasons.
 ISBN-13: 978-0-89272-710-0 (trade hardcover : alk. paper)
 ISBN-10: 0-89272-710-1
 [1. Snowmen--Fiction 2. Winter--Fiction. 3. Tourism--Fiction.] I. Stevens,
Helen, ill. II. Title.
 PZ7.K5223Mag 2008
 [E]--dc22
                                     2007044892

Typography by the Roxmont Group
Printed in China
FCI 5   4   3   2   1

BOOKS • MAGAZINE • ONLINE

www.downeast.com
Distributed to the trade by National Book Network

Not so long ago, when the world was a gentler place and people were more easily pleased, there lived some plain folk whose small village nestled among the tall pines that hugged the shores of a north woods lake.

They were simple people.

They got up with the sun

and went to bed with the stars.

They planted their gardens in the spring,

tended them loving

and harvested them in the fall.

the summer,

All winter, the villagers kept busy cooking, sewing, and carving musical instruments to play during the cold, dark hours after supper. Still the days seemed endless and gloomy, and the children often became restless and glum.

One particularly long winter, as the children's sad faces pressed against the window glass, the grown-ups began talking among themselves.

"Do you remember when?" the children heard them say. Then their voices dropped to a whisper.

The next morning, the children awoke to a wonderful surprise. Their mothers and fathers, grandmothers and grandfathers, aunts, uncles, and older sisters and brothers were all outside making snowpeople.

When the children saw what they
were doing, they ran outside to help.

At first, they made just a few, but they had such fun that they began to make more and more and MORE, until snowpeople circled the entire lake.

They made singing snowpeople.

They made dancing snowpeople.

They made snowpeople
playing leapfrog

and snowpeople making
snow angels,

snowpeople to climb on

and snowpeople to hug.

They made snowpeople
gliding and sliding,
whirling and twirling.

They made them big and small, short and tall, and everything in between.

Before long, word of the snowpeople spread, and neighbors from nearby villages came to see them.

They hurried home to tell their friends, and soon even more folks were coming to see the snowpeople for themselves. In fact, the little village became known as Snowpeople Lake.

Everyone, it seemed, was delighted by the amazing snowpeople.

For an amazing sight it was—with sunlight sprinkling diamonds on the snowpeople during the day, and moonglow spilling its soft, shimmering sheen over them at night.

It seemed like magic.

All the visitors were welcome at Snowpeople Lake.

The villagers gave their new friends mittens, scarves,
and quilts to keep them warm on their outings.

They played music to entertain them. And they prepared wonderful meals for everyone to enjoy together. Finding joy in such simple things, visitors often lingered longer and went home happier than they had expected.

Surely it was the magic of the snowpeople!

Then, sooner than anyone thought possible, winter winds became warm spring breezes and the villagers prepared to greet the new season.

One day, when it was too early to be spring but too late to be winter, a group of visitors arrived to see the snowpeople.

As usual, the villagers were delighted to welcome their new guests. But everyone's delight soon turned to dismay when they went out to the lake and saw the snowpeople beginning to melt!

One dancer had already lost her shoe. Then a snow angel lost her wings, the tumblers lost their tumble, and the smallest of the snowpeople vanished altogether.

"We came to see the snowpeople, and now they're melting!" complained one visitor.

"Is it really worth it to go to so much effort to make something that disappears so quickly?" asked another visitor. "We have traveled such a long distance—all for nothing, it seems!"

But the villagers just smiled, and one old woman stepped forward, holding her grandchild by the hand.

"I'm not sure you understand," she said, kindly. "The snowpeople never really leave us. Things change, but nothing is ever really lost. All of life, including each one of us, is continually changing and renewing itself.

"The spirit of the snowpeople is present in the melting snow as it runs to the lake. It lives in the water and in the mist as it rises to the clouds, to return again as showers in spring, dewdrops in summer, frost in fall, and snowflakes in winter. These are the seasons of life, and we celebrate them all. This is the magic of the snowpeople."

Some of the visitors did not seem to understand. They grumbled and mumbled and hurried away, shaking their heads at the foolishness of such simple people. But, touched by the woman's words, many others lingered, staying to help the villagers sow their spring gardens.

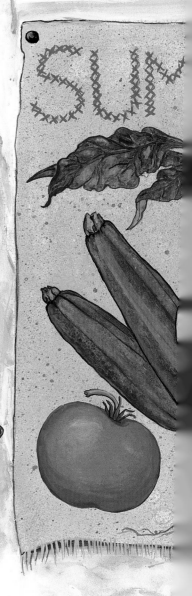

Then they visited agai to help tend the beet

Together they planted the early spinach and peas, leeks and lettuce.

rots, tomatoes, and
uash in summer

and harvest the apples and pumpkins and
grapes and corn in the fall.

And when cold, icy winds brought winter back to
the lake, the visitors returned to join the celebration
as snowpeople sang and danced, whirled and twirled
beside the lake once more.

The End